MAX EHRMANN

desiderata

A SURVIVAL GUIDE FOR LIFE

A SURVIVAL GUIDE FOR LIFE

MAX EHRMANN

desiderata

EBURY PRESS
LONDON

desi

First published
in the UK in 2002 by
Ebury Press
Random House
20 Vauxhall Bridge Road,
London SW1V 2SA

Random House
Australia (Pty) Limited
20 Alfred Street, Milsons
point, Sydney, New South
Wales 2061, Australia

Random House
New Zealand Limited
18 Poland Road, Glenfield,
Auckland 10, New Zealand

Random House
South Africa (Pty) Limited
Endulini, 5A Jubilee Road,
Parktown 2193, South Africa

The Random House Group
Limited Reg. No. 954009
www.randomhouse.co.uk

A CIP catalogue record for
this book is available from the
British Library.

Desiderata © 1927 by Max
Ehrmann. All rights reserved.

Permission by Robert L. Bell,
Melrose,Ma. USA 02176,
End material pp 51-55 used
with the kind permission of
Richard Dowell.

ISBN 009188909X

erata

Concept and picture editing by Steve Barnett

Design by Martin Joyce, Thoughtfields and Steve Barnett

Printed in China

10 9 8 7 6 5 4 3

Acknowledgements
The publisher wishes to thank the following for their assistance in the publishing of this book:
Robert L. Bell; Gene Vaughn; Professor Richard Dowell; Getty Images; Imagesource; Photobank Image Library NZ; Vigo County Public Library, Terre Haute.

Photographs in this book are used with the permission of:
GETTY IMAGES: p10 © Jon Bradley/Getty Images/Stone; p14 © Victoria Pearson/Getty Images/Stone; p18 © Darren Robb/Getty Images/Stone; p25 © Gandee Vasan/Getty Images/Stone; p26 © Ron Krisel/Getty Images/Stone; p33 © Kaz Mori/Getty Images/Image Bank; p35 © Marc Schlossman/Getty Images/Stone; p37 © Klaus Lahnstein/Getty Images/Stone; p42 © Andy Sotiriou/Getty Images/PhotoDisc; p44 © Getty Images/Stone; p46 © Philip Lee Harvey/Getty Images/Stone. IMAGESOURCE: pp2-3, 9, 16, 21, 23, 29, 30, 38, 41, 49. PHOTOBANK IMAGE LIBRARY NZ: p13.

desiderata

Go placidly amidst the noise and haste, and remember what peace there may be in silence. As far as possible without surrender be on good terms with all persons. **Speak your truth quietly and clearly; and listen to others, even the dull and ignorant; they too have their story.** Avoid loud and aggressive persons, they are vexatious to the spirit. **If you compare yourself with others, you may become bitter or vain, for always there will be greater and lesser persons than yourself.** Enjoy your achievements as well as your plans. **Keep interested in your own career, however humble; it is a real possession in the changing fortunes of time.** Exercise caution in your business affairs; for the world is full of trickery. **But let this not blind you to what virtue there is; many persons strive for high ideals; and everywhere life is full of heroism.** Be yourself. Especially, do not feign affection. **Neither be cynical about love; for in the face of all aridity and**

disenchantment it is perennial as the grass. Take kindly the counsel of the years, gracefully surrendering the things of youth. **Nurture strength of spirit to shield you in sudden misfortune.** But do not distress yourself with imaginings. Many fears are born of fatigue and loneliness. **Beyond a wholesome discipline, be gentle with yourself.** You are a child of the universe, no less than the trees and the stars; you have a right to be here. **And whether or not it is clear to you, no doubt the universe is unfolding as it should.** Therefore be at peace with God, whatever you conceive Him to be, and whatever your labours and aspirations, in the noisy confusion of life keep peace with your soul. **With all its sham, drudgery and broken dreams, it is still a beautiful world.** Be cheerful. **Strive to be happy.**

MAX EHRMANN

Go placidly
amidst the noise and haste, and remember what **peace** there may be in silence.

As far as possible
without surrender
be on good terms
with all persons.

Speak **your truth** quietly and clearly; and listen to

others, even the dull & ignorant; **they too have their story.**

Avoid

loud & aggressive persons, they are vexatious to the spirit.

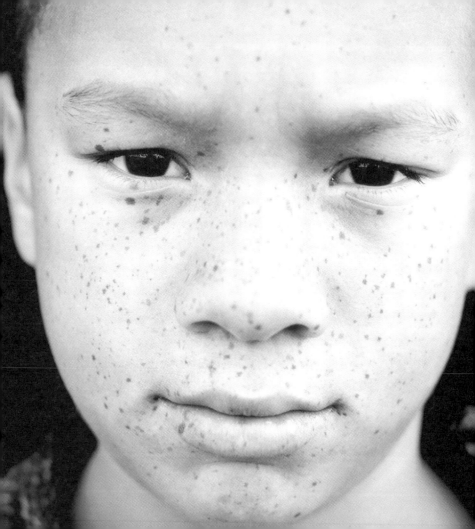

If you compare yourself with others, you may become bitter or vain,

for always there will be greater and lesser persons than yourself.

Enjoy

your achievements

as well as your plans.

Keep
interested in your own career, however humble; it is a **real possession** in the changing fortunes of time.

Exercise caution

in your business affairs; for the world is full of trickery.

But let this not blind you to what virtue there is; many persons strive for high ideals; and **everywhere life is full of heroism.**

Be yourself.

Especially, do not feign affection.

Neither be cynical about

love;

for in the face of all aridity
and disenchantment it is
perennial as the grass.

Take kindly the counsel of the years, gracefully surrendering the things of youth.

Nurture

strength of spirit
to shield you in sudden
misfortune.

But do not distress yourself with imaginings. Many fears are born of fatigue and loneliness.

Beyond a wholesome discipline, be gentle with yourself.

You are a child of the universe, no less than the trees and the stars; you have a right to be here.

And whether or not it is clear to you, no doubt

the universe is **unfolding as it should.**

Therefore **be at peace** with God, whatever you conceive Him to be, and whatever your labours & aspirations, in the noisy confusion of life keep peace with your **soul.**

With all its sham, drudgery and broken dreams, it is still a **beautiful** world.

Be cheerful.

Strive to be happy.

'Insight and serenity;
above all serenity'

Max Ehrmann

To find *Desiderata*'s origins one must travel to the Hoosier state of Indiana, down Interstate 70, to the western border where the Wabash River swings southwest before snaking its way down to meet Ohio.

There, in Terre Haute, one will find a few people who still remember Max Erhmann, the attorney turned philosopher-poet who wrote *Desiderata* in 1927. He was a man who, in his own words, 'could never belong to anything', but who ultimately was true to himself and to the goals he set up for himself.

Max Ehrmann was born on September 26, 1872, the fifth and last child of German immigrant parents Maximilian Ehrmann and Margaret Barbara Lutz. His father, a cabinetmaker for the railroad, provided his family a comfortable home, but more significantly, he gave his children an example of integrity and devotion. Max recalled after his father's death that, 'He was a diligent, loving father and he did all in his power to show us the true path of life – industry, honour, and the forward look. My mother once told me she had never known him dishonourable in word or deed.'

In this close-knit family a love of the arts flourished. The church also was a compelling force and thus began the spiritual questions that Ehrmann would ponder for a lifetime. Though he would move more and more toward a humanistic position, Ehrmann never lost his reverence for 'Jesus the philosopher' or his faith that 'the universe is unfolding as it should'.

Ehrmann graduated DePauw University at Greencastle, Indiana, where he became the editor of the *DePauw Weekly*. The university's

desiderata

wooded campus, intellectual aura, and pervasive tranquillity stimulated his idealism and brought him to what was perhaps the pivotal decision of his intellectual life.

Following his graduation in 1894, Ehrmann entered the School of Philosophy at Harvard University where he spent two years specialising in law and philosophy, before returning to Terre Haute to lead the precarious life of a poet and philosopher. Though he worked steadily and somewhat successfully at his art, ultimately he accepted the sad truth that literature, at least for a time, would have to be an 'avocation'; he turned to the practice of law and became deputy prosecuting attorney, a position he held for two years. However, as time passed, literary pursuits consumed more and more of his time and energy. The inevitable result of his double life was illness in the form of typhoid fever. It was during his convalescence that Ehrmann wrote *A Prayer*, which, like *Desiderata* later, would become a message of hope for thousands.

After his recovery, Ehrmann returned to the business world as a lawyer and credit manager for his brothers' overall manufacturing firm. Yet always he looked forward to the day when he could devote himself wholly to his writing – the kind of writing he wanted and needed to do, not necessarily the kind that would sell. Instead of compromising his literary ideals and become a hack writer, he remained at the factory for ten years, devoting his nights to literature and saving his money for the day that he would be financially free. 'To preserve my soul,' said Ehrmann, 'I wrote late into the night hours.'

By 1912, at the age of forty, Ehrmann had

abandoned the world of business and devoted himself entirely to literature, the only pursuit he had ever found truly rewarding. As he told an interviewer toward the end of his life, 'At DePauw I contracted a disease which I have never shaken off. The disease was Idealism.' In a three-room apartment, Ehrmann lived the last thirty-three years as he had always wanted to live, as a poet and philosopher.

'The world in miniature' is how Ehrmann described his 'native city' of Terre Haute. Ehrmann prized the friendships and tranquillity he found there. Chatting with acquaintances, offering advice and encouragement to young writers, lunching with Indiana State Teacher's College professors, exercising on the archery range, or just sitting placidly on a bench in Deming Park – these were activities that gave his life

meaning, that filled him with the inner peace and human understanding so characteristic of his writing: 'In large cities one's views are diffused; here none escapes one's microscope. The histories of many lives I have seen unfold year after year. Here there is romance and heroism – the whole drama of human life . . . Let me drive out of myself the universal madness to be elsewhere in search of the joy of life, for the joy of life resides within oneself.'

A few days before Christmas in 1921 Ehrmann wrote in his journal: 'If in an hour of noble elation, I could write a bit of glorified prose that would soften the stern ways of life, and bring to our fevered days some courage, dignity and poise – I should be well-content.'

That 'bit of glorified prose' was to be

desiderata

Desiderata which Ehrmann would write six years later when aged fifty-five. Written, he said, for himself, 'because it counsels those virtues I felt myself most in need of'. The poem travelled in his pocket for months, and it was his guide in striving for simplicity, sincerity and serenity. Like so many of Ehrmann's works, *Desiderata* grew out of an inner need and was shared with others wishing similar comfort and assurance.

In December 1933, Ehrmann used *Desiderata* as part of a Christmas greeting sent to his friends. Later, during the Second World War, Merrill Moore, an army psychiatrist, wrote to Ehrmann that he had distributed an estimated one thousand copies of *Desiderata* over the years while in civilian practice in Boston and requested and received permission from Ehrmann to distribute *Desiderata* to soldiers as part of

his army care. 'I think you should know,' Moore wrote, 'that nearly everyday of my life I use your very fine prose poem *Desiderata* in my work – here I have found your philosophy useful . . . I use *Desiderata* liberally and always find it helpful . . . it should be bottled and sold as Dr Ehrmann's magic soul medicine!'

During his final years, Ehrmann's life and work were the subjects of numerous articles and reviews, and, on Sunday, June 24, 1945, Terre Haute formally paid tribute to Ehrmann when testimonials to his work as a poet and his genius for friendship were given by musicians, college teachers, artists and friends at a gathering in the city. Following his death just three months later, on September 9, tributes were written by those who knew him best. The most extensive is *Max Ehrmann: A Poet's Life*, written by Bertha

King Ehrmann, his long-time friend and his wife during the final year of his life.

In death as in life, however, Max Ehrmann did not come by his fame easily. From the mid-1950s the authorship of *Desiderata* became obscured.

The poem's appeal had seen it much copied and passed from hand to hand. In one such instance the rector of a Baltimore church, wishing to share *Desiderata*'s inspirational message with his congregation, distributed copies of the poem that included a notation to the church and its founding date in the seventeenth century. Gradually the belief grew up that the poem dated from that time, adding to its charm and appeal.

Desiderata gained huge popularity on posters during the 'make peace, not war' movement of the 1960s. The poem found its way to San Francisco's 'flower children' who embraced it as a supposedly centuries-old affirmation of love and peace. Printers eagerly ran off many millions of posters and handbills.

In the years since, however, the true origin of this famous poem has been reclaimed, with Max Ehrmann and *Desiderata* assured of an eternal niche in American popular literature. *Desiderata*'s appeal continues undiminished, its formula for happiness – a gentle urging to be at peace with God and life – of universal appeal.